The Lonely Grey Dog at Number 6.

Tammy and Jake find out about

Love and Loyalty

Catherine Mackenzie

© Catherine Mackenzie 2005
Published by Christian Focus Publications
Geanies House, Fearn, Tain, Ross-shire,
IV20 1TW, Scotland, UK.

Cover illustration by Dave Thompson
Bee Hive Illustration
All other illustrations by Chris Rothero
Bee Hive Illustration.

Printed and bound in Denmark
by Nørhaven Paperback A/S

ISBN 1-84550-103-9

For Lydia, Esther, Philip,
Lois and Jack.
The Lord's steadfast love
endures forever.

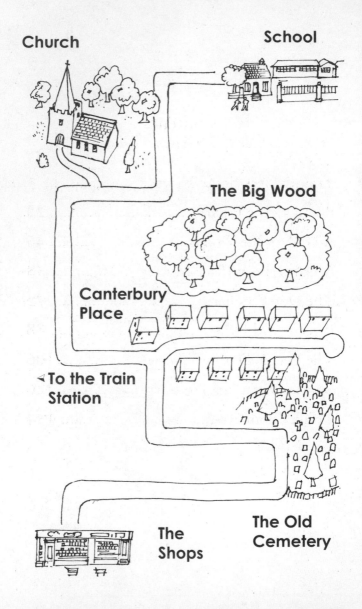

Church

School

The Big Wood

Canterbury
Place

◄ To the Train
Station

The
Shops

The Old
Cemetery

Contents

Tammy Gets Some News 7

Being a True Friend 28

A Walk in the Woods 46

A Canterbury Place Mystery 58

The Dog Catchers 72

Joyce's Old Desk 88

The Secret Drawer 106

Sports Day and a Big Surprise 126

Think about it 154

Tammy Gets Some News

It was early on Saturday morning. Number 11 Canterbury Place was pretty quiet. Dad and Jake were enjoying a lie-in. Mum had been in the garden trying to get the Morris Minor to start. Her hands were smudged with grease and a spanner stuck out the back of her dungaree pockets. Tammy, as usual, was up early and was on her way down the stairs when the post arrived. Tammy picked up the letters and made her way to the kitchen, shuffling through them as she went.

Tammy was quite a good letter-writer and often wrote her Gran in Scotland and her cousin, Jen who was getting married this summer. In fact, the wedding was only a couple of weeks away and the whole MacDonald family were invited.

As Tammy made her way into the kitchen, she spotted the last letter in the pile and smiled. It was from Jen – she was sure of it. There was an Edinburgh postmark on the front and the writing looked liked Jen's. She had very curly writing with lots of loops and swirls. But the letter was for

Mum and Dad. So Tammy put it at the top of the pile. She wanted her mother to open it first. 'I wonder what news Jen has this time?' Tammy thought.

Mum came through from the sitting room and exclaimed, 'Oh, a letter from Jen! Your Auntie Lynn said that she'd be dropping us a line. I wonder what she wants?' Mum slit open the envelope with a butter knife.

Tammy peered over Mum's shoulder for a better look. 'Be patient Tammy,' Mum smiled, 'I'll read it out to us both. Now let's see, *"Dear Auntie Jane and Uncle Mark...,"* and then she said, 'Oh my! Tammy! What a bit of news I have for you!'

Tammy stared at her mum's excited face. 'What is it? What is it? Tell me Mum,' Tammy urged once more.

'Jen wants you to be a bridesmaid! My goodness, that is at short notice though,' Mum declared. Hands on her hips. 'That girl is so like her father. Talk about leaving everything until the last minute!'

Tammy didn't care. Jake woke up to the sound of her squeals and groaned. Mr MacDonald who was just out of the shower laughed when he heard Tammy's excitement from downstairs. 'Come on, Jake,' he joked, as he knocked on his young son's door. 'Get up and get showered. You won't get any peace until Tammy's told you her news.'

Jake sighed. Mum often celebrated special occasions with a cooked breakfast – and judging by Tammy's squeals this might just be one. Jake trudged along the corridor to the bathroom where the sink

and his toothbrush were waiting. When he was all freshened up he made his way down the stairs. He'd been right. His nostrils tingled. Mum had grilled bacon and sausages as a treat. There were also hot tomatoes and mushrooms sizzling away in the oven. Jake smiled, 'It must be one of Mum's non-diet days. She has cooked the full works for breakfast. Whatever news Tammy has it must be good.'

'It's not every day a MacDonald family member is asked to be a bridesmaid,' Mum announced, as Jake came through the kitchen door. 'Listen to this…,' she exclaimed. *"We are sorry it is at such short notice, but when I thought about it*

11

I realised what a good idea it was to have Tammy – my cousin and pen pal – as a flower girl at my wedding. Even though she is a lot younger than the other bridesmaids' I know she will do really well. So, if you don't mind, could you arrange to get Tammy measured. Mum is making all the dresses and they are nearly finished, so it won't take long to get Tammy's clothes sorted out. Mum says sorry that you've got such a disorganised niece but that it really is all right as she can sew like lightning."*

'As long as she doesn't sound like thunder while she's doing it,' Mum exclaimed, before carrying on with the letter. "*If you could all come up and stay with us for a few days beforehand that would be great. We'll do a final fitting for Tammy as well as catch up on family news.*'"

Tammy butted in, 'What colour will the dresses be Mum?'

As Mrs MacDonald showed Tammy some samples of material that had been tucked in with the letter, Dad began to work out how they were going to get up to Edinburgh on time without breaking the bank. 'Train tickets will be too expensive. I think we should drive. It will be good to spend a few days in Edinburgh. I'll be able to show the kids round my old hometown.'

Mum nodded her head and smiled, 'But it's such short notice. Jen is just like your brother. If it weren't for Auntie Lynn nothing would get done in that family. And since we're talking about driving, that car of mine is finally through. We can't keep spending money on it, but do we have to get to get rid of it?'

 Dad sighed. 'You and that old car. I don't know. Let's deal with it after we get back from Edinburgh. There's too much going on just now.'

Jake smirked as he looked at his parents. Mum was a bit untidy looking and the day had hardly started. Dad would be out in the garden soon polishing his blue Ford while mum held her old Morris Minor together with string and sticky-back plastic. Between them they were working out the route to Edinburgh by car. Mum was scribbling down notes as she went. 'We just have to get organised!' she exclaimed. Dad grinned, 'Finally,' he laughed. 'The MacDonalds get organised. I never thought it would happen.'

Mum smiled at his joke and carried on scribbling while Dad reminded her to take extra time off work, cancel the papers and book a guesthouse.

It was funny to see Mum and Dad working together like this. Dad was always organised. He was so organised, he even hated surprises, as they were things he couldn't plan for. Mum, on the other hand, loved surprises. She liked to do something brand new and unplanned. Jake realised that both his parents were quite different from each other. Yet they both got on pretty well. Tammy and Jake were different too. Tammy was always first up in the morning. As soon as the birds began to sing Tammy would be up and dressed. Jake was not like that at all. Saturdays were a treat because he was allowed a long lie. Jake's family was made up of some very different people.

He thought about Mum's brother, Uncle Matthew and his wife Auntie Clare. They didn't have any children but Uncle John and Auntie Lynn had three - Jen, Paul and Sarah. They were Tammy and Jake's cousins but all three of them were older than Tammy and Jake.

There was a picture of the Edinburgh MacDonalds as Mum called them on the mantelpiece in the sitting room. It had been taken a long time ago when Jen had still been at school.

Uncle John was holding Jen in his arms - something he couldn't do now without a struggle. There were so many different people in Jake's family... some were organised, some weren't, some liked to cook fancy meals and some preferred pizza. He'd even heard that Auntie Lynn loved green beans - whereas Jake detested them.

'Everybody's different,' Jake thought to himself, 'but we all love each other and get on quite well.'

Jake thought that this probably had something to do with God. The MacDonald family tried to follow God's Word and obey him, and Mum and Dad had brought up Tammy and Jake to love him too. It was good to have cousins, and family who followed God. Mum always said that you had to work hard at being a family. It wasn't always easy.

Just then Mum began to rake around one of the kitchen drawers. From the back of a drawer she pulled out a long tape measure and held it up against Tammy. She measured across her back and round her middle and down her arms and all over. Then she exclaimed, 'Tammy, love, you've grown ... quite a bit!'

'Of course!' Tammy exclaimed. 'I'm no baby anymore!'

Mum sighed. 'But it only seems like yesterday you were over there in a high chair throwing yoghurt at everybody!'

Jake laughed and so did Tammy and as Mum looked at the two of them laughing their heads off, she decided it was a good time to put some new

marks on the wall. By the back door there were blue marks for Jake and red marks for Tammy that showed just how much they had grown over the years. Mum took out the pens and soon there was a new Tammy mark and a new Jake mark.

Just then Jake saw that Mum's face was smiling and looking sad at the same time. 'Isn't it amazing. Jake has outgrown his last pair of trainers; Tammy has shot up several inches and Jen's getting married. It will be one of ours next,' Mum sighed.

Jake almost choked on his toast. 'Mum – don't be ridiculous!' he exclaimed. The very idea of Tammy or him getting married was silly. Tammy, however, didn't think so as she immediately started humming the bridal march and glided gracefully down the corridor.

The next day was Sunday so Jake looked forward to going to church. It was a time to tell God that he loved him. Jake's friends, Daniel Conner and Dave Johnson, would be there too. Jake smiled when he thought about Daniel being his friend. It hadn't always been like that. Jake remembered how Daniel had bullied him in the past.* It had been after his other friend, Timothy, had left to live in another town.

Just then Jake remembered that he was supposed to visit Timothy during the holidays. As they were driving down the road to church he asked Mum if it would still be all right to do this now that there was a wedding on. Mum nodded. 'Timothy's home is half way between here and Edinburgh. So we could drop you off after the wedding. You could stay there

for a few days and then his parents could drive you home. Timothy seems to have settled in now, thankfully.'

'Yes,' Jake replied. 'He's stopped all that smoking nonsense, which is good.'* Jake felt relieved that Timothy was happier now. At first he had made some bad friends in his new school. Timothy had been smoking and even stealing things from the local newsagent. But Jake had been a good friend and had helped Timothy through it all. However, there was still a small problem. Jake wasn't sure if Timothy loved the Lord Jesus or not. Jake was glad that he had given his own heart to Jesus Christ. He remembered how he'd broken Mum's vase and blamed it on the family dog. He'd felt so guilty about it. Jake had known he'd done wrong - and it was only when he'd told the truth and asked Jesus into his life that he'd began to feel better.

For Mum's birthday the other month he'd bought her a new vase which she loved. It had cost quite a bit of his pocket money but Jake was glad that he'd done it.

As he walked into church, Jake thought about how Jesus had been beaten and spat on and made fun of. He'd been nailed to a cross and even abandoned by God, his Father. Jesus had to suffer death and all these things because of sin. Someone had to take the punishment, and Jesus had been

 the only one good enough to do it. Jesus had come back to life, and because of what Jesus had done it was now possible for Jake and others to be friends with God. As Jake sat down beside his parents he thought about all the good things God had given him... love, forgiveness, heaven and a life that would last forever when he died, a life that would be with Jesus.

Jake's mouth broke into a big smile as the singing began. It was such a wonderful thing to be loved by God. He had to make sure that his friend Timothy knew about it.

'If Timothy doesn't love Jesus he really needs to,' thought Jake. 'Having a friendship with Jesus is the most important

 thing. What sort of friend am I to Jesus if I don't tell others about him?' Jake asked himself. 'What sort of friend am I to Timothy if I don't tell him such important news?'

After the church service was over Tammy told everyone her good news. It wasn't long before the whole church knew that she was going to be a bridesmaid. Joyce, the Sunday school teacher, was almost as excited as Tammy. 'Do you like weddings or something?' Jake asked her.

'Of course I do,' she replied. 'I love them. It's a celebration. In fact, I think heaven is going to be like a wedding – a great big celebration. When I go to a wedding or a party I think, "This is good, but heaven is going to be even better."'

Jake looked at Joyce and asked, 'How many weddings have you been to then?'

She stopped to think. 'Oh, I'm not sure. Probably twenty. My sister's wedding was the first one I went to. I was a bridesmaid at that. Then there was my best friend from school and my cousin Dave. Uncle Jeremy got married the year after that. He must have been sixty when he got married.'

'Really?' Jake asked, astonished.

'Yes … old people get married too. In fact, all round the world people get married in different ways. In some countries the ceremony lasts for over a week and the parents arrange everything even down to who their child gets married to.'

'Are the children happy about that?' Jake asked, puzzled.

'Sometimes. They can end up being

happy and it works out well. In this country the bride and groom usually choose for themselves who they are going to marry and don't worry Jake ... The wedding you are going to will only last a few hours. You'll have to tell me all about it when you get back.'

Jake shook his head, 'I won't need to. Tammy will do that.'

Joyce smiled. 'She probably will, but Jake did you remember that we're starting the parables of Jesus in Sunday school next week?'

'Yes, all the different stories that Jesus told.'

'Let's do the story that Jesus told about a wedding. I'll make invitations to hand out to the class and we can have a kind of party.'

Jake thought this sounded great fun. 'I'll tell Tammy,' he said. 'Watch out. You'll be able to hear her squeals all the way across the church.'

Being a True Friend

When they got home that afternoon, Mum asked Tammy and Jake to set the table for lunch and Dad was put in charge of the vegetables. It was at times like this that Jake missed Dogger. He'd been very sad when Dogger died and still missed the friendly old dog.* Sundays had always been Dogger's favourite day. There had been

28

plenty of time for a long walk and he had often been given a little bit of chicken or roast beef when lunch was over.

Just then Mum caught Jake looking at where Dogger's basket used to be. She ruffled his hair and sighed. 'You miss him, don't you?' Jake nodded. 'Well, he was an old dog,' Mum pointed out, 'and really sick. Perhaps you'd like to get another one now?' Mum asked.

Jake wrinkled up his  forehead. 'I don't think so. We had Dogger for years. I don't really want to forget about him just yet.'

Mum smiled. 'It wouldn't be forgetting him. But I understand – he was a loyal dog; you want to be loyal to him too.'

Mum then opened the oven to look at

the roast. She breathed in and smiled. 'It smells great. The potatoes look ready. Tammy, put the salt and pepper on the table. Jake can fill a jug of water and then we'll sit down and thank God for the food.'

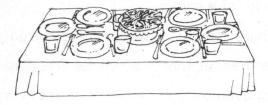

Soon they were all sitting down at the table and Dad said the prayer. 'Thank you, Lord, for this food. Thank you that you care for us. Thank you for Jen and Phillip, the man she is going to marry. May they love you and be loyal to you and to each other. In the name of your son, Jesus Christ, Amen.'

Jake and Tammy passed the vegetables around and soon everyone was tucking in. Just then, Dad asked Tammy, 'What story were you doing in Sunday school today?'

Tammy swallowed a mouthful of corn, 'We have just finished doing the story of David,' she said.

Jake joined in. 'A few weeks ago we heard about how God chose David to be king even though his older brothers were bigger and stronger than him.'

'Then,' Tammy said, 'we read about how God helped David fight Goliath, who was an awful lot bigger and stronger than him.'

'This week,' Jake explained, 'we were learning the story of how God helped David fight against another enemy – King Saul.'

'Yes,' Dad nodded his head. 'If I remember rightly, Saul didn't want David to become King even though it was what God wanted. The people liked David more than Saul, and this made Saul jealous. But David had one good friend, didn't he?'

'I know,' Tammy exclaimed, 'Jonathan. Read the story again. It's a good one.'

'That's a great idea. I'll get the Bible. It's sunny enough to have our deserts out on the lawn.'

Later, as Dad was in the garage finding a deck chair to sit on, Jake saw that Mum was staring at the back of the garden.

'What are you looking at?'

She shook her head and put her sun specs on again. 'I must be seeing things, Jake,' she said. 'I thought I saw something disappear under the hedge over there. It looked like a tail or something. I don't know...?'

'A squirrel?' Jake asked, puzzled.

'No, it was a lot bigger than that,' Mum said. 'With the glare of the sun I didn't get a close enough look.'

Jake saw that Tammy was hanging around by the hedge and was now trying to peer over it. He called out to her. 'Hey Tammy... what was that?'

'What was what?' she yelled back.

'That thing Mum saw crawling under the hedge.'

Tammy just shrugged her shoulders and wandered back down to the house. Jake sighed, and went to investigate for himself.

'Tammy is dreaming too much about the wedding,' he muttered.

As Dad was getting the Bible Jake looked at the back hedge. There was nothing there except a big hole. 'Something could crawl through there,' Jake thought. 'I'll mention it to Dad later on.' But just then Mum came out with a tray of ice-cream sundaes for everyone and the thought went clean out of Jake's head.

It was a great day for just sitting in the sunshine. Mum and Dad were on the deck chairs and Tammy and Jake sat on cushions on the grass. Dad opened the

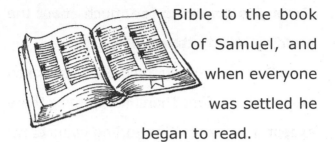

Bible to the book of Samuel, and when everyone was settled he began to read.

'David was a good musician, wasn't he? Before I start can either of you remember what instrument he played?'

'The harp,' Tammy answered.

'That's right. It was a stringed instrument. In the Bible there is a book called the Book of Psalms. It is a collection of poems and songs, and David wrote quite a few of them. Now, because he was a well known musician, the palace officials would ask him to play music for the King. Saul suffered from bad moods and soothing music made him feel better. However, one day David was playing his harp when King Saul decided to throw a spear at him. Thankfully David darted out of the way. The spear hit the wall instead, and David fled from the palace as fast as he could.

'He could see that King Saul wanted to kill him and that he couldn't risk being at the palace any longer.

'Now, David's wife, Michal, was a daughter of King Saul. Instead of helping her father she was loyal to her husband. 'If you don't escape tonight you will die,' she told David. So Michal helped him climb out of a window. She placed an old statue in David's bed and put some goats' hair pillows at the top. With a blanket covering the statue, the goat's hair pillows looked just like someone's head. When the Palace guards came to look for David, Michal showed them the bed and the goat's hair pillows and said that David was far too sick to go to the palace just now.

'When Saul found out that Michal had deceived him he was very displeased. He asked her why she had done this? Michal lied and said that David had threatened to kill her if she didn't help him.'

'That was mean of her,' Tammy exclaimed.

'It was,' agreed Dad. 'She shouldn't have lied. She wasn't being faithful to her husband. But David had another friend who helped him escape and didn't lie about him either. He was King Saul's son, Jonathan. But was he the heir to the throne?'

'What does heir mean?' Tammy asked.

'Joyce told us, Tammy. Don't you remember?' Jake went on to explain. 'An heir to the throne is someone who will become king or queen. When a king or queen dies one of their children becomes king or queen instead. Jonathan was King Saul's son.'

'So Jonathan was supposed to become the king after Saul died?' Tammy looked a bit puzzled.

'Not in this case,' explained Dad. 'God chose David to be King instead. Jonathan understood this but Saul didn't. Jonathan knew that it was important to obey God, but Saul just did not want David to become king. Instead Saul plotted to kill him. Jonathan decided to do all that he could to help David. He showed real loyalty to his friend even though his own father was against him.'

'What is loyalty Dad?' Jake asked.

Dad thought for a second. 'Fetch a

dictionary, Jake, will you? We'll see if that will help us.'

Jake ran into the house and very shortly he was running back outside with the dictionary in his hand. Jake flicked through the pages and came across the word loyalty.

'A feeling of friendship or duty towards someone,' Jake announced.

'Look up the word loyal too,' Mum suggested.

'That means to be faithful to one's family, country or government,' Jake replied.

'Right then,' Dad said. 'Jonathan was loyal to David. He stuck up for him. Jonathan was a true friend. That's what loyalty is. It's showing true love even when times are hard. When David wanted to find out what Saul's plans were, he asked Jonathan for help. What happened next?'

Jake knew the answer to this one. 'Jonathan told David to hide himself beside a heap of stones. Jonathan then went back to the palace to find out what his father's plans were. Later he came back to where David was hiding and shot three arrows into the distance. It was a secret message that told David to run for his life. If Jonathan hadn't shot the arrows far it would have meant everything was safe, but because they had been shot into the distance David knew he really was in danger.'

'That's right, Jake,' Mr MacDonald nodded. 'It was a sad day for David and Jonathan. The two friends had to say goodbye, and they would never see each other again as long as they lived.'

Tammy was curling a golden curl around one of her fingers and shielding her eyes against the glare of the sun. 'I liked the bit about Jonathan being a true friend to David. It's important to have good friends.'

'That's right. Jonathan was a friend to David even though he would become king instead of him. Jonathan wasn't jealous – he loved David and he loved God. But did you notice that the dictionary missed out something?' Dad asked Tammy and Jake.

Jake thought for a minute. 'I know. It didn't mention God. We should be loyal to our family, our country and God.'

'That's right! In fact, let's put that in the proper order - God, family and country. God should be the most important person in our life.'

Mum then reminded Tammy about Jen's wedding. 'The minister will tell the bride and groom that they should remain faithful to each other. That means the same as being loyal. Husbands and wives should be loyal to each other. Michal was loyal to David when she helped him escape, but then she lied about David and eventually her father made her marry someone else. We don't know if she was happy to obey her father or not. But it is wrong for someone who is married to love someone else when their husband or wife is still alive.'

'I remember when your mother and I got married,' Dad smiled. 'The minister told us to say the words 'until death us do part.' That means that husbands and wives are to stay married until one or other of them dies. A marriage is for life. That's the way God has planned it.'

Tammy then sat up on the cushion and looked her parents in the eye. 'But that doesn't always happen, does it?'

Mum shook her head sadly. 'No, it doesn't. It's like everything else in life. If we let sin spoil things, it will. Sin can make friends fall out; it can make parents and children disagree and fight; it can even make husbands and wives fall apart.'

Mum rubbed a sore spot at the back of her neck. 'You know that I'm always on about loosing weight and being healthy. It can be difficult to do the right thing. I might eat chocolate instead of fruit or read a book instead of going for a walk. If you want to pass exams you need to study.

 If you want to ride a bike you have to practise. If you want to have a good marriage you have to work at that too.'

Tammy shuffled closer to Mum and asked, 'How do you do that then?'

'You have to put others first before yourself.

Jesus, Others, You.

The first letter of all these words spells joy. To have a joyful marriage that is what you need to do – put Jesus first and then others and then you.'

Tammy nodded and Dad leaned over to give Mum's neck a bit of a rub.

'Was that what it was like for you and Mum when you got married?' Tammy asked. 'Did you both love Jesus first?'

44

Mum smiled and grinned at Dad. 'Yes, I am so pleased that I fell in love with your dad. I knew that he loved Jesus most of all and that was the most important thing.'

Just then an idea popped into Tammy's head. 'Let's look at your wedding photos,  Mum. I'd really like to see them.'

Dad laughed, 'Good idea, Tammy. But I think Jake and I will go for a walk. How about it, son? What would you prefer, a walk in the woods or photographs?'

'The woods,' Jake exclaimed, and ran off to grab his walking boots.

A Walk in the Woods

Jake rummaged around the bedroom and eventually found his walking boots under a pile of clothes in the corner. Then Dad and Jake strode off towards the woods. Jake decided to ask Dad a question.

'Joyce isn't married, is she Dad?'

'No, she's single. I don't think she's even going out with anyone.'

Jake nodded, thoughtfully. 'Why isn't Joyce married? She's really nice. She's fun. She doesn't look ugly.'

Dad laughed out loud. 'Oh Jake, lots of people don't get married for lots of reasons. When I was a student at university I prayed to God to give me a good wife. Then one day I thought that maybe God didn't want me to get married.'

'Did you feel upset about that?' Jake asked his Dad.

'A little, maybe ... but I wanted to please God. I realised that it was very important for Christians to love and marry other Christians.'

'Why is that?' Jake asked.

'Well marriage is an important relationship. God made the first man and the first woman to be companions, to be

man and wife. It was one man and one woman. If you love God, and you want to have a truly close relationship with your husband or wife, then they need to love God too. At university I had already given my heart to Jesus. I knew that if I fell in love with a girl who didn't love God then that would hurt my relationship with him.'

'How come?' Jake asked.

'Well, I need to find a picnic table.'

'There's one over here,' Jake called out. 'Behind that large oak tree.'

They ran over to the tree where Mr. MacDonald helped Jake to stand on top of the picnic table. 'Now,' he asked Jake, 'do you think it will be easy for you to pull me onto that table? Give it a try.'

Jake braced himself and pulled on his Dad's arm, but nothing happened.

'I can't do it!' Jake gasped.

'O.K. then. How easy do you think it will be for me to pull you off that table?'

Jake braced himself, but with one quick tug he had stumbled off and his Dad was swinging him around in the air.

In between their bursts of laughter, Jake and Mr MacDonald heard a voice calling out, 'What are you doing?' It was Daniel Conner from Number 17.

Dad put Jake on the ground and, wiping some sweat from his brow, he flopped down beside him.

Daniel scrambled over the fence and then headed over to chat with them.

'I'm explaining to Jake how it's important that Christians should only marry Christians,' Mr MacDonald explained.

Daniel looked puzzled. Mr MacDonald then said, 'You saw how difficult it was for Jake to pull me on to the table.'

Daniel nodded. Jake had tried hard, but he hadn't even moved his dad one inch.

Mr MacDonald continued, 'However, it was easy for me to pull Jake off.'

'That's true. But then you are bigger than him,' Daniel declared.

'Yes, you have a point there. So we'll do it again. This time Daniel can get on the table.'

With one leap Daniel was up on top of the picnic table.

'Try and pull Jake up with you, Daniel. Let's see how you do. Give it your best shot,' Mr MacDonald smiled as he stood back to watch.

Daniel didn't manage. And when Jake tried to pull Daniel off he struggled, but eventually Daniel tottered and had to jump into a pile of nearby wood bark.

'I was sure I'd be able to pull Jake on to the table,' Daniel grumbled.

'Well, let me tell you why Christians should marry other Christians,' Mr MacDonald explained. 'An old man called Charles Spurgeon was talking to a young lady in his church. She wanted to marry a young man who didn't love God. She thought that once she married him she would be able to persuade him to come to church. Mr Spurgeon knew that she was mistaken. He showed her how it was difficult for someone to pull another person on to a table but how it was very easy for someone to pull another person off a table. Mr Spurgeon told the young girl that a Christian who is married to a non-Christian will find it very difficult to make the non-Christian follow God. But the non-Christian won't have to  try very hard to stop the Christian from even reading the Bible.'

Jake didn't agree. 'That wouldn't happen to me,' he said.

'Don't be so sure, son,' Mr MacDonald warned. 'A few of my friends used to come with me to church a lot. They read their bibles too, but when they fell in love with a non-Christian they lost interest and stopped hanging around with Christians completely. Sometimes even Christians can make wrong decisions and they can stop listening to God. If you start listening to other people instead of God then lots of bad things can happen in your life. If you love Jesus ask him to make you love him more and more each day. It's such a shame when Christians turn away from following Jesus. Thankfully, Jesus never turns away from those he has saved. But I want you two boys to think about the women you might marry one day.'

Jake and Daniel looked at each other and sniggered.

'Now come on, be serious. You might get married one day, so remember that marriage is for life. It's not like joining a club or a gym. You can join something like that one week and stop going the next. Marriage is different. When men and women get married God wants them to stay married until…'.

'Death us do part,' Jake replied.

'That's right. Choosing a wife or a husband is an important decision. You should pray about it. Daniel's auntie Joyce may get married some day. If she does, she should marry someone who loves God. I am sure that's what she wants.'

Daniel nodded. 'I used to wonder why Auntie Joyce wasn't married. When I was little I was always asking her if she wanted a husband. She used to say that as soon as she found the right man I'd be the first to know.'

Jake laughed, 'If she does get married she'll make you her pageboy. I think you'd suit a little blue suit and velvet shoes.'

Daniel then jumped to his feet and said, 'Not as much as you'd suit some wood bark down your neck, Jake MacDonald.'

And with that the two boys ran off towards the pond leaving Mr MacDonald to wander along at a quieter pace.

Later on Mr MacDonald decided to head back to the house. Jake and Daniel agreed to take the long way home by going to the other end of the big wood. Jake thought they would keep an eye out for Dave who might be trying out his new roller blades. 'He lives on that street at the back of ours – the one on the way to school.'

Daniel nodded, 'Yeah, I know the one. Did you know that he used to live in Joyce's house?'

Jake nodded. 'I remember that. So his family is

responsible for that really untidy garden we had to sort out.'*

Daniel grimaced. 'It was full of weeds wasn't it?'

'Yeah. That was hard work.'

Daniel then looked a bit thoughtful. 'I remember how we talked about how sin takes over people's lives like weeds take over a garden. Sin can choke all the goodness out of life sometimes.' Daniel scratched his head a bit. 'I've been wanting to sort out some wrong stuff in my own life.'

'You love God, don't you?' Jake asked.

'You know I do. He's great and he loves me.'

'Well, God is the only one who can deal with sin. Jesus has paid the price for your sin.'

'But why do I still do things wrong?' Daniel asked.

'Mum told me that we are not going to be perfect until we go to heaven to be with Jesus. So at the moment all we can do is ask God to help us to stop sinning. When we are tempted to sin we are supposed to run away from what is tempting us.'

Daniel nodded his head. 'It's hard work, isn't it?'

'Mum says that lots of things are hard work. Being in a family or being married can be hard work. You have to put others

first, but make God the most important person of all. God never said that being a Christian would be easy.'

Daniel sighed. 'Too right – digging gardens is much easier.'

Jake smiled, 'But heaven is going to be fantastic - The best celebration ever... it's going to be great!'

A Canterbury Place Mystery

Just as Jake and Daniel arrived at Canterbury Place Jake had a strange feeling something else was bothering Daniel.

'Spit it out, Daniel, what's wrong?'

Daniel scratched his head. 'Your Dad said that God wants men and women to stay married for life. But what if they don't get married in the first place?'

Jake stopped in his tracks. Now this was a difficult question. 'What do you mean, Daniel?'

'Well your cousin is getting married. My cousin and his girlfriend decided not to get married, and now they have a baby and live in a house together. I was just wondering what God thinks about that?'

Jake thought for a second, 'I've a funny feeling that it's not what God wants – but I'll ask Dad about it when I get home.'

Just then Jake spotted Tammy walking by herself. Daniel decided to head home while Jake ran to catch up with her. 'I thought you were looking at photos,' Jake exclaimed.

Tammy blushed. 'I can do what I like,' she announced gruffly. 'I don't have to tell you everything.'

Jake shrugged his shoulders. Tammy might be growing up, but sometimes this just meant that her temper was getting shorter.

'Chill out, Tammy,' he said. 'You can keep your secrets if you want,' Jake smiled.

Tammy smiled back, looking a bit sheepish. For a minute Jake thought she was about to tell him something – but then she just ran inside. Jake followed her and then thought that now was as good a time as any to ask his parents about Daniel's question. Jake knew that it was a tricky one.

Mum spoke up first. 'You know, Jake, that God designed marriage for men and women? It is best for children to be born in families where they have a mother and a father. It is also best for children to be born in families where the parents are really committed to each other. In one sense a marriage is an official agreement, it's a legal promise that two people will love and be with each other for life.'

Dad then joined in the conversation. 'But sometimes children don't always have both parents around. We know that bad things happen sometimes. People die, and so children can lose a parent. Sometimes husbands and wives split up and the family falls apart. Sometimes people choose not to get married. But it is best for a man to love one woman and a woman to love one man. That's God's rule and he wants us to follow it. He wants a husband and a wife to be loyal to each other.'

Mum added, 'That doesn't mean that other types of families don't work. Sometimes they do. It just means that a mum-and-dad type of family is the best.'

Dad nodded. 'But a mum-and-dad family can have problems too. It's important to remember that whatever sort of family you are in you can have a better family life if you trust in Jesus.'

'But Daniel's cousin loves his girlfriend and they have a baby too. Doesn't that count for something?' Jake asked.

'Yes, Jake, but if the mother and the father don't trust or follow God this means that their life is built on very shaky ground. Without God you have nothing that truly lasts. Without God your family life can collapse. But more importantly, without God you won't have eternal life, will you?'

Jake nodded his head. He understood that.

'If Daniel's cousin wanted to obey God and follow him he would get married. Getting married is not just a way of showing your boyfriend or girlfriend how much you love them, and it's also more than a legal document or promise.'

'What is it then?'

'Marriage should be about two people going to God and asking him to help them in their married life. They promise God, and each other, that they will love and look after each other until they die. When someone refuses to get married they are ignoring God.'

'You see, Jake,' Mum pointed out, 'some people love each other and want to live together. A boy might say, 'I love this girl so much I don't need to get married to her. She knows how much I love her.' But this is disobeying God. Marriage is about keeping promises to God and to each other.'

'So what do I say to Daniel about his cousin?'

'Well,' Dad explained, 'you can tell him that God's Word says that marriage is to be honoured. So his cousin should get married. It might be difficult for Daniel to say this to his cousin though. It is often very hard to tell other people in your family that they are doing something wrong.'

'That's right,' agreed Mum. 'We should pray that Daniel is able to tell his cousin about Jesus. It might not be the right time for him to tell them to get married, but he can always tell them about Jesus.'

Jake leaned back in his chair and remembered the discussion about loyalty. 'If Daniel's cousin got married he'd be showing loyalty to his girlfriend.'

'Exactly,' said Dad. 'Daniel's cousin  probably loves his girl friend. He probably thinks that he will never leave her, but life with other people can be difficult.

'When difficulties come, it is often good for people to be married. It sometimes means that they try harder to stay together.

'But even people who are married fall out and leave each other. That's when some people get a divorce.'

'Do you know what a divorce is, Jake?' Mum asked.

Jake said, 'Kind of.'

'Well a divorce is really just a legal document that says a marriage has ended. People get divorced for different reasons. Sometimes both people decide to end the marriage. Sometimes one person decides that they love someone else. Do you remember what the Ten Commandments says about that?'

Jake scratched his head a little. 'The seventh commandment says that you should not commit adultery. So that means that you shouldn't leave your wife and get another wife.'

'That's right,' Mr MacDonald said. 'The Ten Commandments also say that you shouldn't covet or want someone else's wife. So it's against God's law to even think about being disloyal. In my opinion, the important thing that keeps people together when they are married is a love and respect for God and each other.'

Jake had another question though. 'People who don't believe in God can show love and respect to each other too?'

'Yes,' said Mum. 'God is amazing. He gives good things to people who believe in him and to people who don't. The Bible tells us that God sends rain to the fields of godly people and ungodly people. He gives good gifts to everyone. He can give the gift of a good marriage to people who  don't actually trust in him. If people ignore these gifts though, and do not thank God for them, it will be the worse for them on the judgement day.'

Jake knew that the judgement day was the day when all God's people would be with God forever – but those who did not trust in Jesus would be sent away forever. Jake looked very sombre. It was a difficult thing to think about. Mum reached over to give him a cuddle.

'We often hurt other people when we sin. Sometimes married people hurt each other and need to forgive each other. When we love God in the way that we should, we will love our families in the way that we should. In fact if you love God you will love your family and friends more than anyone or anything. But I'd like you, Jake, to go upstairs and drag Tammy away from her wardrobe. She has been up there all afternoon trying to match up her shoes with the material for the bridesmaid's dress! Oh … and Joyce called in when you were out to give us some chocolate cake. We can have a slice of that for our afternoon tea.'

'So the diet starts tomorrow?' Mr MacDonald winked.

Mum just smiled politely and told him to put the kettle on.

Jake ran up the stairs. Mum didn't know that Tammy had been out that afternoon, or maybe she had forgotten? Jake didn't worry about it though. Tammy was allowed to go and play on the street if she wanted to. Jake called through Tammy's door that there was chocolate cake in the kitchen and then he ran back downstairs. As they were all enjoying the cake, Mrs MacDonald remembered the story that Joyce had told her that afternoon when Jake and his dad were out on their walk.

'Joyce came back from church this morning and her bin had been tipped over. She thinks that an animal did it. There were some left-over scraps dropped on the driveway. Perhaps it was the animal I thought I saw disappearing under the hedge?'

Jake then told Mum about the hole in the hedge and she wrinkled her brow a bit. 'Well, whatever it is - we should keep an eye out.'

Jake nodded, 'I'll tell Daniel and some of the others. They might have heard something.'

'Yes, Jake,' Dad agreed. 'That's a good idea.'

Before Jake went to bed that night he had a quick look out the bedroom window. But there was no sign of anything. He thought about what fun it would be to solve a mystery. He wondered what sort of animal it was. Maybe it was the same animal Mum had seen disappear under the hedge?

Just then though, in the distance, Jake heard a howl, loud and long. 'We don't have wolves in Canterbury Place?' Jake asked himself. He stopped to listen again. Could he have been mistaken? As there was no longer any sound Jake closed the curtains and jumped quickly into bed. 'I'm not scared,' he said to himself rather loudly.

The Dog Catchers

Monday morning arrived and Jake wondered if anyone else had heard the creepy sounding howl the other night. He decided not to mention it. Mum and Dad would probably think it was just a bad dream. And besides, he wanted to investigate the situation for himself. Daniel and Dave could help out too. They would be like explorers or wild animal hunters.

'Maybe we will get our photos in the newspaper?' Jake thought to himself.

The only photos that Tammy was interested in were wedding photos. She had seen wedding pictures of Mum in high heels and now she wanted to wear high heels at Jen's wedding. Mum said, 'Absolutely not! You're tall enough without the help of high heel shoes. And besides, you'll be on your feet all day. If you wear silly shoes like that you'll have blisters.'

'You wore them to your wedding Mum!'

'I know. My feet were killing me!'

As Jake flopped down at the breakfast table he realised Mum was right. Tammy was getting quite tall.

'She can reach the cereal cupboard by herself now,' Jake noticed. He wondered if he would always be able to call Tammy his 'little' sister. 'How come she's growing so quickly?' Jake puzzled. He was still the older – nothing would change that – but what if little sisters could grow taller than their big brothers? 'I'll have to eat more vegetables,' Jake decided. 'I'll even eat green beans if it means staying taller than Tammy,' he sighed.

Thankfully you never eat green beans at breakfast, not even in the MacDonald house. So  Jake settled down to a bowl of cereal.

Just as the dishes were being cleared Dad clattered in the back door a bit flushed looking. 'Our mystery dog is back.'

'What do you mean?' Mum asked.

'Our bin was knocked over and papers were all over the grass. It's definitely a dog. There are paw prints on the flower beds to prove it.' Dad sighed, as he slumped into a chair with a cup of tea. 'If it happens again I'll phone the police.'

Tammy gently whispered, 'The police?'

Mum brushed Tammy's hair into a ponytail. 'Well if there is a stray dog you have to be careful. Let's hope its owner will find it soon.'

Just then the doorbell rang. 'That will be Daniel,' Mrs MacDonald said, as she looked at the clock. Jake had already rushed to the door. 'Tell him to come in,' Mrs MacDonald called after him. 'We'll have the Bible time together. Daniel, have you had your breakfast?'

'Yes thanks, Mrs MacDonald,' Daniel replied. 'I've eaten.'

Tammy came in with the Bible, Mrs MacDonald leafed through it as Mr MacDonald sat back with his cup of tea.

'What will we read about today?' Daniel asked.

'Well, I thought we could read about people who were loyal to God. God has given us so much. We should be true friends to him. We should use the gifts that he has given us to tell others about him.'

'How do we do that then?' Daniel asked.

'Well, God has given you a healthy body and a good mind. He might ask you to be a missionary and take the news of Jesus Christ to a far away country?'

'Or he might ask you to become a preacher,' Mr MacDonald suggested. 'You could use your mind to learn about God and then tell others about him.'

'Someone who is good with words could become a journalist and write stories in the newspapers. God uses all sorts of people to tell others about himself,' Mum explained.

'In fact,' Mr MacDonald said, 'you can be a preacher, a missionary, a teacher or a scientist. If you love, obey and worship God you are being faithful to him. God gives us abilities and strengths, but his greatest gift is Jesus Christ.'

'His son,' Daniel added.

'That's right,' agreed Mum. 'So I thought I'd start our Bible reading today with a story about Jesus. Throughout the gospels we read about Jesus and his friends.'

Daniel put up his hand, 'What do you mean by gospels?' he asked.

'That's just another name for the first four books of the Bible: Matthew, Mark, Luke and John. It's in these four books in the Bible that we read about the life of Jesus from his birth through to his death and resurrection, and then when he went back to heaven.'

Daniel nodded. 'I know about the resurrection. That's when Jesus came back to life.'

'That's right. Well Jesus had friends and enemies. When he was going around the country preaching about God, there was quite a crowd of people with him. Jesus spoke about how it was only through him that people would get eternal life. He spoke in the open air and by rivers, on mountaintops and inside buildings and houses. One day some people had gathered together to worship God. Jesus told them that he was 'the bread of life' and that through him they could live forever. Many of Jesus' followers did not understand what he was talking about. Jesus told them that they could not really be his followers unless God, his Father, allowed them to be.

Just then many people who had been following Jesus decided to leave him. They weren't really friends of his at all. But Jesus still had his twelve disciples with him. He asked them if they wanted to leave too.

Peter replied, "Lord, where else can we go? You alone have the words of eternal life. We believe in you and know that you are the Holy One of God."

Mrs MacDonald put away the Bible and turned to the children. 'Jesus knew who trusted in him and who didn't. He even knew who would betray him. Jesus knows our hearts too. He knows if you are faithful. He knows if you love him or if you don't. If you love him, it is God that has helped you to do this. If you do not love him, then you must ask God for his help. It is only God who can change your heart and make you love Jesus. It is only God who can make your love for him grow stronger every day. It is only God who can make us love himself and love others in the way that we should.'

Mr MacDonald then closed the Bible time with a prayer. 'Lord God, thank you, for your holy son, Jesus Christ. Thank you for sending him to die in our place on the cross. Help us to love and trust in you. Help us to be faithful to you in work and at school. Forgive us for our sins, in the name of Jesus. Amen.'

'Right,' Mrs MacDonald called out. 'Find your school bags and Jake remember your spelling book. I saw it on the couch earlier on! Tammy stop looking at yourself in the mirror or you'll be late for school.'

As Jake grabbed his spelling book from

off the couch, and Tammy took one last look in the mirror, Jake told Daniel about the mystery dog. 'Friday is the last day of term...,' Jake thought out loud.

'And the sports day too,' Daniel reminded him as they all headed out the door.

'So if we get together with Dave after school and set up a look out in Joyce's garden... we could camp out in the garden and keep watch?'

'Shouldn't be a problem,' Daniel agreed. 'I think our parents will be fine about us staying up late. If we take it in turns to watch, we'll be able to sleep for some of the time.'

Jake grinned from ear to ear. This was beginning to sound like fun, he thought.

Daniel pointed out that wheelie bins were difficult to topple over. Jake thought about this. 'Mum thinks it was because our bin was really full. Perhaps Joyce's was too. If a bin is really heavy sometimes it doesn't take much to push it over.'

Daniel agreed that was probably true, and he remembered that Joyce had been doing a clear-out recently, so perhaps her bin had been full too. 'So what will we use to trap this dog?' Daniel asked.

'We could tempt it with some food,' Jake suggested.

Daniel agreed. 'That's a good idea, Jake,' he said. 'That dog is probably hungry.'

'Right then, I'll ask Dave what he's up to. Do you think you can get round Joyce and your parents without them finding out too much? They'll only want to stop us if they find out we're trying to trap a dog.'

Just as Daniel was nodding his

agreement, he remembered something. 'Good job you told me to speak to Joyce. I've just remembered that she's asked me to speak to you. Joyce bought a desk at the yard sale at Number 6 the other week. She needs help to shift it upstairs, and my dad says that he'll give her a hand if he can get two strong lads to help him. I reckon he means us.'

'That's fine,' Jake smiled. 'We're strong. Does she want us to come after school today?' Jake asked, as he flexed a muscle on his arm.

'Yes, she does. She knows we've got super-human strength,' Daniel grinned.

After the school day was over, Tammy and Jake walked home with Daniel again. It had been a busy day with a spelling test and art lesson for Tammy and sports practice

for the boys. There was so
much to do in school
at this time of year,
but it was a lot of
fun. Jake and Daniel
were chatting about
who would win the sprint when Daniel
nudged Jake in the arm. In a loud whisper
Daniel said, 'Look over there!'

Jake turned in time to see a long grey
body slink round the corner into a side
alley. Jake knew that some houses kept
their bins in that alley. Both boys decided
to make chase. Tammy looked as though
she wanted to stop them, but Jake turned
to her and said, 'It's all right. We'll be fine,
but don't tell Mum whatever you do.'

Tammy just shrugged her shoulders and
left while the two boys ran round the corner.

There was no sign of any animal, let alone a dog. But something had been trying to get at the bins... one of the smaller ones was already on its side. Thankfully it had been empty, so there was no rubbish to clear up.

As they stood by Number 11 chatting about it, Tammy listened in. 'We've got to catch that dog,' Jake exclaimed. 'It's going to be us or the police.'

'That's right,' agreed Daniel. 'I reckon it will be easy to trap it.'

Tammy glared and stamped her foot. 'Leave it alone!' she yelled and ran back to the house. Jake called after her, 'Remember what I said about not telling Mum.'

Jake and Daniel agreed to meet at Joyce's later

to shift the desk and Daniel then headed home.

'It's not dangerous, Tammy,' Jake whispered to his sister later. 'I'm certain about it.'

'You don't need to tell me that,' she snorted. 'And believe me, I won't tell Mum or Dad.'

Jake muttered 'thanks' as he and Tammy both brought out their homework to do together.

Joyce's Old Desk

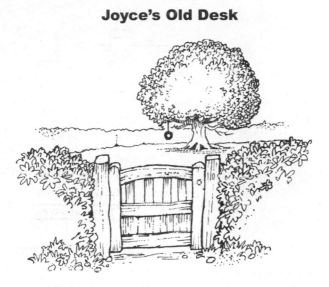

Tammy didn't mention the dog to anyone. In fact, she didn't say much at all. After she cleared away her books she ran outside to practice her skipping.

As Jake was finishing his homework he heard Tammy on the driveway. Her sneakers went thump, thump against the tarmac and he could make out the swish of the skipping rope, as it cut through the air. Tammy's voice rang out loud and clear as she counted her jumps. 'Sixteen, seventeen, eighteen....' Then there was a scuffle and a mutter as Tammy tripped on the rope and scolded herself. Tammy then dragged her rope behind her into the kitchen. Her cheeks were flushed and her blonde hair was sticking out all over the place.

'Time for tea,' Mum called, and ushered the two children to the table. 'Dad's working late. If we're going to go to this wedding he has to get a lot of paperwork done before we go. Pull up your seats, and Jake, you say the prayer this time, will you?'

Jake closed his eyes,  'Dear God, thank you for this food, thank you for the good weather. Help us to be true friends to Jesus. Amen.'

Something at the back of Jake's mind made him think that he should not be planning things behind Mum's back. 'I'm not lying,' he thought. 'I'm just not telling everything.' Jake knew Mum wouldn't see it that way. He pushed the guilty feeling aside and tucked into his tea.

After Mum had served up a quick tea of pizza and salad the conversation came back to the wedding. Mum thought that Jake needed a new tie for the occasion. 'Just don't pick an old grand-dad tie,' he pleaded.

Mum laughed, 'Don't worry, Jake, I'll pick something modern looking. Now finish your food and help me wash up. Joyce phoned earlier about shifting that desk. Mr Conner and Joyce will do the heavy lifting, but you and Daniel need to open the doors and things. Tammy can go with you. There are some old boxes of stuff that Joyce bought at the yard sale. She thought Tammy could help her sort through them.'

Tammy smiled. Jake was relieved that her good mood had come back and he laughed, 'You won't find any treasure, Tammy. That old man at Number 6 didn't own much. All he had was books, a radio and a grumpy old dog....'

All of a sudden Tammy was glaring at him once again. 'What have I done now?' Jake wondered.

Once Jake and Tammy were over at Joyce's it didn't take Jake long to see why Joyce needed help. The desk was huge. 'How are we going to get that thing up the stairs?' he asked Daniel.

'Dad says he knows what he is doing,' Daniel said.

And he did. Mr Conner took the drawers out of the desk and then turned it on to its side. Daniel and Jake were told to go ahead and make sure that the study doors were open. 'Keep your eyes open and shout directions to us as we're going up these stairs,' he reminded them. 'I don't want to bump into anything.' Between them Joyce and Mr Conner were soon heaving the desk up the stairs to the study. Once the desk was in position, Mr Conner set off for home and Jake and Daniel put the drawers back in place. It was now ready for Joyce's papers and correspondence.

Jake ran a finger over the leather covering. It was worn and scratched from years of use. He wondered how many letters had been written on that desk and who the different owners had been over the years. It was pretty old.

When Jake and Daniel came down the stairs again, Tammy was going through the boxes. She was sorting out some old china ornaments and there were some old photographs and frames on the carpet too. Daniel began to chat to Joyce about putting a tent up in her garden overnight.

'Really?' she said, surprised. 'Whatever for?'

Daniel looked a bit sheepish. Jake could see he wasn't going to be able to keep this secret. With Daniel's blushes and Jake's silence Joyce knew they were planning something. 'You're up to something. I can tell. What's your secret?' she demanded.

Jake and Daniel knew there was nothing they could do now so agreed to share with Joyce their idea about trapping the dog.

'And how were you going to trap it exactly?' she asked, puzzled.

'We thought we would tempt it here with some dog meat.'

'Uh huh,' Joyce said. 'That might work, but there is no way that I am going to have you boys trying to trap what might be a very hungry and frightened animal. You might get hurt. However, I am not against you camping out and keeping watch. As soon as you see anything you have to tell me.'

'How are we going to do that without frightening the dog off?' Daniel exclaimed. 'We won't catch it if we have to run up the stairs first to wake you up.'

'Well, it just so happens that I have a couple of walkie-talkies.'

'What?' Jake and Daniel said together.

'I used them last year when I was on a walking trip with friends. Some of the group would walk ahead of the others to set up the camp for the night. But we kept in touch with these things....' Joyce pulled two yellow walkie-talkies out of a drawer.

'Perfect,' Daniel exclaimed. 'We'll radio in to you as soon as we see it and then you can come with us – adult supervision. Our parent's can't stop us now.'

Joyce sighed. 'Now boys... parents want to make sure you are safe; you know that.

But I think this will be quite safe if you follow my rules.'

Daniel and Jake said that they would, and that they would make sure that Dave would too.

Just then there was the sound of the front door closing. Jake looked around. 'I think Tammy's headed off home. She must have got bored. Sorry about that, Joyce. Will I tidy up the boxes for her?' he asked.

'Just put them over there on the sideboard, Jake love,' Joyce asked.

Jake lifted up the boxes and, as he did so, he spotted something that had been shoved far down inside the wastepaper bin. It was quite a nice photograph frame. 'Why is Joyce throwing this out?' Jake wondered.

Jake picked it up and looked at it closely. 'Daniel, what do you think of this?' he called out. Joyce and Daniel went through to see what it was that he had found. 'Recognise anything?' Jake asked.

Daniel peered closer and then he gasped. 'That's our mystery dog! I'm sure of it.'

Jake nodded. 'It's the same colour, the same size....'

Joyce said, 'Well, if you're right, then that dog belonged to the old man at Number 6.' Jake and Daniel grinned at each other. It seemed as though the mystery was almost half solved.

Joyce looked thoughtfully at the photograph. 'How strange... I never saw that dog when I was at the sale. There was a kennel... but somebody bought that and took it away with them.'

Daniel wondered about asking why Joyce had thrown the picture in the bin ... but it was none of his business anyway. When all the work had been done Jake and Daniel both left Joyce's house with strict instructions to ask their parents permission about the camping trip; and they weren't to hide any of the facts.

However, when Jake's mum heard that Joyce was in charge she wasn't worried at all. 'Do you want me to make up something for a midnight feast?' she offered. Jake thought that was an excellent idea. It was a good thing really to tell your mum what you were up to... especially if she was going to organise food.

That night the MacDonald family sat down to read the Bible before going to bed. Jake wondered what story they would read tonight. In the morning Mum had read a couple of verses from Psalm 136. 'Give

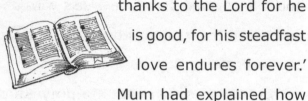 thanks to the Lord for he is good, for his steadfast love endures forever.'

Mum had explained how steadfast meant the same as faithful or dedicated. It was something that would not be moved. They had been talking a lot about people who were loyal and faithful, so it was good to realise that God was more faithful than anyone. His love lasted forever.

Dad found the chapter he was planning to read and cleared his throat.

'I thought I would read another story

about David the King. You've done his story in Sunday school, but you stopped just before he becomes King. Lots of things happened to David after that. He fought many battles but made some mistakes too. He coveted someone else's wife and murdered the woman's husband in order to marry her.'

'That was so wrong,' Tammy said, shocked.

'You're right,' Dad nodded solemnly. 'David was truly sorry for his sin though, and turned away from it. He asked God to forgive him. In Psalm 51 David asks God to give him a clean heart. "Have mercy on me, O God, according to your steadfast love; according to your abundant mercy blot out my transgressions. Wash me thoroughly and cleanse me from my sin."

'Now, you know what steadfast means, don't you, Tammy?' Mum asked.

'It means faithful and dedicated. It means you cannot be moved. But what does the word "abundant" mean and what does the word "transgressions" mean?'

'Here are two more new words for you then, Tammy.' Mum wrote them in a notebook so Tammy could see how they were spelled. 'Abundant means lots. If you had an abundant supply of shoes – which you have – that would mean you have a huge number of shoes. Transgressions is another word for sins – disobeying or not obeying God.'

Dad got Tammy and Jake to shuffle closer so that they could see the words for themselves in the Bible. 'You see, David did something that is very wrong, but he still knew he could ask God for help. He knew that God forgives, but he also knew that God hates sin. God's love will not be moved, he is full of love and mercy, and because of that he was willing to help David get rid of his sin. God is willing to help us too. David asks God to wash him thoroughly and cleanse him from sin. What do you think about that?'

Tammy thought for a second and then said, 'Sin is like a dirty stain. A smudge can spoil your face. A stain could spoil a dress - sin spoils my life. But it's God that cleans us.'

Jake nodded. 'Mum cleans the floor to get rid of the dirt. If the floor wasn't cleaned it would get dirtier and dirtier. If God doesn't sort out our sin our lives get worse and not better.'

Dad leaned back against the couch and continued with the Bible lesson. 'That's right. But sometimes people who sin and ignore God just go on sinning and ignoring God. They think nothing of it. That can be hard for us to understand.'

'But if we aren't forgiven sin stops us from going to heaven,' Jake said.

'Yes, that's exactly right, Jake, and we must remember that sin is in all our lives. Many people think that they are better than other people. That is called being proud.

Some people say, 'I'm a good person because I've never killed anyone.' But Jesus warns us that if we are full of hate towards someone, this is the same as murder. Perhaps you have thought about hitting someone? This means that in your heart you really want to kill them. Even though your body hasn't done it, it is still sin and we need to say sorry to God for our sinful thoughts and longings.'

Jake looked at his dad with a troubled expression. 'I've done that, but I keep seeing more and more sins in my life!'

Dad nodded his head. 'It's like this, Jake, when we give our lives to Jesus, the Holy Spirit shows us our sin. The closer we get to Jesus Christ the more we see our sin. To show our loyalty to God we should ask him for help. We need help to defeat sin. God is the only one who can do this.'

'Often we show loyalty by doing things for others,' Mum said. 'So in our family or school we take on more responsibility. We can do more things for God too, but one of the ways we show loyalty to God is different. You can show loyalty to God by depending on him more and more.'

'That's right,' agreed Dad. 'God wants us to come to him with our problems just as little children come to their parents with all their needs.'

'Now, it's time for bed,' said Mum. 'Get some sleep. We want you on good form for

the sports day. It's the wedding after that, so we're going to be in for a busy time.'

Jake started to talk about the high jump competition that he had entered and Tammy began a long description of her bridesmaid's dress.

Dad yawned, and said, 'Get to bed both of you. There's plenty of time to get excited about these things tomorrow.'

The Secret Drawer

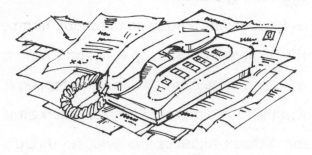

The following morning Jake was up and about quite early. But Tammy, as usual, had been up before him. As he came down the stairs she was coming in the front door. 'Where have you been?' he asked, puzzled.

Tammy just shrugged her shoulders yet again and headed for the kitchen.

Jake sighed – then he felt hungry – so he headed for the kitchen too. Mum was on the phone speaking to Auntie Lynn about the Tammy's dress.

When it was time to go to school, Tammy ran on ahead to meet up with some friends at the end of the road while Jake stopped at Number 17 to pick up Daniel. As he waited for Daniel to pick up his bag, he thought over the Bible verses from that morning. Dad had read another verse that mentioned the word steadfast... but this time God was telling his friends and those who loved him to be steadfast. God was encouraging them to be strong, and to keep going  even though people tried to make things difficult. Jake remembered how Daniel used to tease him about going to church. That had been difficult. But Jake was really pleased now that God had changed Daniel's heart. Now Daniel was really keen about going to church, and he'd become a Christian too. Jake repeated the verses to Daniel when they were walking down the street, 'But thanks be to God who gives us the victory through our Lord Jesus Christ. Therefore be steadfast, immovable, always abounding in the work of the Lord, knowing that in the Lord your work is not for nothing.'*

'I thought it was funny when I heard the words - always abounding in the work of the Lord. I thought it sounded like someone was on a trampoline bouncing or bounding about. But Mum explained that it was another word like abundant. It means that we should do lots of work for God and let God do lots of work in us. We've a really important message to tell people,' Jake reminded Daniel. 'It's the good news that Jesus Christ loves us and wants to save us from our sin. It is only by believing in Jesus Christ that we will be saved from sin and from hell.'

Daniel nodded in agreement. 'I know that it can be hard being a Christian in school. But it's even harder being a Christian when your parents aren't.'

'Your Dad's been going to church though,' Jake pointed out.

'Yes, but he doesn't come that often. Mum comes with me when she feels well enough.' Just then Daniel stopped short. In the distance, somewhere in the woods, there was a long, loud howl. 'It's the dog,' the two boys declared together.

'He sounds hungry,' Daniel whispered.

'He's going to be ready for our trap on Friday then,' Jake whispered back.

The two boys nodded. Jake and Daniel could hardly contain themselves through the long day at school. When it was over, the two boys and Dave Johnson sat outside Joyce's and worked out what to do. Daniel fetched some sleeping bags; Jake went to his mum's store cupboard for some of Dogger's left-over dog food. He had expected to find quite a few tins - but he could only find a couple now. 'Mum must have given them to the dog pound,' he thought. Jake came back over with some

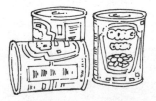 biscuits, the tins and an old tin opener and dog dish. These and some torches

and the walkie-talkies were all put into the shed for the big day. There was no point in putting up the tent just yet. There were two whole days until Friday. Jake wondered how he would be able to stand it.

That night, during the Bible time, Mum began to read another story about someone who showed loyalty to Jesus. 'I'm reading this story from the gospel of John chapter 12.' She leafed through the pages until she found the right one.

'Here we are reading about a woman who showed great loyalty to Jesus. Her name was Mary of Bethany. She was a good woman who loved God and believed in his son, Jesus Christ. She loved to sit and listen to what Jesus taught. She knew that finding out about Jesus was the best thing that she could do.

'One day she wanted to show Jesus just how special he really was. She had a very expensive jar of ointment. It was so expensive it would have cost a whole year's wages. Mary broke the jar above Jesus' head and let the ointment pour out and soak into his hair. There was so much ointment it trickled all the way down his head and over his shoulders. It dripped down his cloak and onto his feet. The smell was amazing. It spread all the way through the house.

The others in the room were astonished. Why did she do it? Judas, the disciple, was very annoyed. 'Why didn't she sell it so  that the money could be given to the poor?' he asked. But Jesus told him to be quiet. 'You will always have the poor with you,' he said. 'But you won't always have me with you. She has done this thing to prepare me for my burial.'

Jake looked puzzled. 'Judas was really annoyed, wasn't he?'

'Yes,' Mum agreed. 'He was in charge of the money bag you see. The disciples and Jesus travelled around together, so any money they had was put into this bag. Judas was in charge of it, but he also stole from it. That's why he was annoyed at Mary. He realised that if she had sold it and given the money to Jesus, he could have stolen that money from Jesus and the others.

But Mary wasn't thinking about money. She was thinking about Jesus. She knew, somehow, that he was going to die. She knew that he was the Son of God. She wanted to show Jesus how much she loved him. She wanted to show the world that they should love him too.

The following morning, as Jake was going to school, he kept  thinking about Mary of Bethany. She had really loved Jesus and had been willing to give everything to him, all that she had. It must have cost her a lot of money to buy that perfume. She didn't mind if Judas was mean to her. She knew that Jesus was the important person in that room.

At school that day Jake did some more sports practice. He had entered the high jump and had been practising for weeks.

Dave was going in for the sprint and needed a lot of practice too. Jake and Daniel had been helping him do exercises to strengthen his legs, and had even timed him as he ran home from school.

That afternoon after school Jake and Daniel raced Dave home on their cycles as he ran back through the woods. Dave's time was even better than his last one, and that had been pretty good. So they all thought he stood a good chance of winning on Friday.

As Jake and Daniel wandered home discussing tactics for increasing Dave's speed, Tammy waved at the boys from the doorway of Joyce's house. 'What are you doing there?' Jake asked, puzzled.

Tammy replied, 'Joyce asked me over to look at something? You'll never guess...

Joyce has found a secret drawer.'

Jake and Daniel were astonished. Both boys rushed up the stairs to Joyce's study where she was kneeling under the desk with a surprised look on her face.

Everyone knelt down for a closer look.

'Have you managed to open it yet?' Daniel asked.

'Not quite – something is sticking. Pass  me the scissors, Daniel love. I'll see if I can unblock it with that. Something is jammed at the back.'

As Joyce tried to unblock the drawer, Tammy explained what had happened.

'Joyce was polishing the desk when she noticed that under the rim there was something that felt like a button or a small handle. She pressed it and heard a strange

noise. When Joyce bent down to see where the sound had come from, she noticed that there was a small drawer half open just at the side here.'

Tammy knelt down again and pointed to where Joyce was sticking the letter opener. Just then the drawer sprung open and a small dusty letter and a notebook dropped out.

'That's what was jamming it,' Joyce exclaimed, as she came out from underneath the desk. 'Now let's see what we've found. Jake, phone your mum and tell her what's happened. She might like a look too. I think it's an old diary.'

Mrs MacDonald loved surprises and couldn't believe Joyce's luck at having a secret drawer of her very own. 'I used to dream about those as a kid,' she exclaimed, when they were all sitting in Joyce's study. 'It's like something you would read about in an adventure story.'

Joyce nodded. 'I think I'll leave the diary for now, but look at this letter….'

Mrs MacDonald picked up the faded old letter and began to read.

"Dear Donald,

We heard this morning that Carrie has been involved in a serious accident. It happened on Tuesday, and her father and I are leaving on the next train. She is in hospital in London. We only hope that we *will be on time, and that the doctors will be able to do something. She was driving the ambulance when the bomb hit.*

We will write when we know more, my dear. We know how much you love her, and we have been so looking forward to your marriage to our lovely daughter.

Be brave and we will give her all your love.

With all our love

Mary and James."'

Tammy, Jake and the others looked quite shocked. It was a horrible letter to read.

Tammy had been hoping for a love letter. Jake had been hoping for a treasure map. Instead, this was the true story of a real wartime disaster.

Joyce lifted up the diary again.

'What's the date on that letter, and where was it being sent to?'

Mrs MacDonald looked again at the letter, 'May 5th and I think it was being sent to someone in the armed forces. I can't make out the person's name, but the letter was sent to a base camp in the south of England.'

Joyce leafed through the diary trying to find a clue about the story. 'I'm guessing he wouldn't have found out about Carrie until sometime near the end of May. But look at this entry for June 8th ... that's some time later. *"Received telegram. Carrie laid to rest May 27th in St. George's cemetery. I will always love her."'*

Joyce wiped a tear from her eye and sighed. Mrs MacDonald shook her head. 'Donald must be that old man from

Number 6. I only knew him as Mr Carter. I spoke to him quite a few times over the years, but he never mentioned this woman once. He never got married... that's about all I can tell you about him.'

Joyce nodded. 'I suppose there was no other person for him but her.'

Jake wasn't sure about that. 'Is there only ever one perfect person that you have to find before you get married?'

Mum smiled, 'I don't know about perfect. Nobody is perfect. But for some people there is only ever one person that they love. Even when that person dies they could never think of marrying someone else. However, other people are very sad for a time but eventually they marry again.'

'Isn't that being disloyal?' Daniel asked.

'No, Daniel,' Mrs MacDonald explained. 'Husbands and wives are to be loyal until death. When someone dies the wife or husband is free to marry again.'

Joyce gently put the letter inside the cover of the diary. 'I'm not sure what to do with this. I don't think it's right to keep it. What do you think I should do?'

'I think you should send it in to the War Museum. They collect stories like this. They might even put it on their web site.'

Joyce decided that she would do that the very next time she was in London.

As Mrs MacDonald took Tammy and Jake home that evening she talked some more about loyalty. 'I hope we always remember what those people did for us during the Second World War. People fought and died so that other people could live. People like Carrie put themselves in danger, so that hopefully one day other people could live in safety.'

'But it is more important to be loyal to God isn't it.' Jake pointed out.

'That's true. But many people who fought during the Second World War were fighting so that we could worship God. They knew that the enemy did not believe in the one true God. In Germany, at that time, there was a German pastor called Dietrich. He fought against those who had taken over Germany. In the end he was put in prison and killed. Other Christians in other countries helped too. Corrie ten Boom from Holland rescued Jewish people and hid them in a secret room.'

'We heard about that in school. During the Second World War Jewish people were killed just because they were Jews.'

'Yes. It is important to realise that loyalty is fine if you are loyal to a good thing. If you are loyal to a country that is doing evil, then that is wrong. Be loyal to God first. If you follow his ways you cannot go wrong.'

That night, Jake lay in his bed looking at the wind blowing in the tree outside his window, he thought about the diary and the letter and the girl buried in a church yard somewhere. He wondered where the cemetery was, and if people left flowers on Carrie's grave. Loyalty could be a hard thing ... sometimes it meant that you had to pay a price. Sometimes it meant that life was difficult and you got hurt. But Jake knew that there was someone who understood that better than anybody. He closed his eyes and thanked Jesus for the loyalty he had shown God, his own Father, by obeying him. Jesus had died on the cross to save his people from their sins. He had been obedient. Jake was really glad that he had.

Sports Day and a Big Surprise

Thursday came and went pretty much like most of the other days that week. There were no more surprises though so Jake and the other boys spent most of their time planning for their night under canvas. Mum made sure that Jake looked out his sports kit and that he cleaned his boots thoroughly.

Thursday evening Bible time was about another person who had shown disloyalty to Jesus. Dad turned to the gospel of Luke.

'In the gospel of Luke there is a story about Peter, one of Jesus' disciples. He boasted to Jesus that he would be with him to the end and would even die for him if he had to. But Jesus told Peter that before the cockerel crowed three times, Peter would deny that he even knew Jesus. This was exactly what happened when Jesus was arrested. Peter did not stand by him. When Peter realised what he had done he cried bitterly. How awful for one of Jesus' closest friends to treat him in this way.

'Now I'm going to turn to the gospel of John,' explained Dad. 'Peter had been disloyal to the Lord Jesus, but when Jesus

 rose from the dead he came to speak to his disciples. He spoke to Peter and asked him, 'Do you love me?'

Peter said, 'You know that I love you.'

Jesus told Peter to look after his sheep and then he asked Peter a second time, 'Do you love me?'

Peter replied, 'Yes, Lord, you know that I love you.' Jesus told him to look after his lambs. Then Jesus asked Peter for a third time, 'Do you love me?'

Peter was hurt that Jesus had asked him the same question three times. He replied, 'Lord, you know all things. You know that I love you.'

Jesus told him again to look after his sheep.

Even though Peter had not been a true friend to Jesus, Jesus wanted Peter to put it behind him and work for God once more. Jesus asked Peter three times if he loved him. Peter had denied Jesus three times. Now Jesus was giving Peter the chance to tell him that he loved him – once for each of the times that Peter had refused to do it.'

Dad put the Bible away and turned to Tammy and Jake. 'God wants us to love him with all our hearts and he wants us to love others just as much as we love ourselves. We wouldn't deliberately hurt ourselves, would we?' Mr MacDonald asked. 'So we shouldn't say or do anything to deliberately hurt someone else. We shouldn't be nasty to our friends. We shouldn't fall out with them or ignore them. We should always treat the people we love with gentleness and respect. We should be good to our parents and loving to our husbands and wives. We should be someone that others can trust as well as love.'

Mum gave Tammy a cuddle, her eyes were drooping and she looked quite tired. 'Ah, Tammy, it's time for bed. Get a good sleep, dear, and you too, Jake. Tomorrow is the last day of term. And it's a busy weekend too.'

And as Tammy padded up the stairs, she muttered 'We're leaving for the wedding on Monday, aren't we mum?'

'Yes dear,' Mum smiled. 'That's all sorted. It's not long now.'

Sports day was a hive of activity. When all the parents started to arrive the school grounds were soon full of races, team sports and other events. Tammy's group came second in the relay race. Jake was third in the high jump and Daniel came second in the long jump. But soon it was Dave's turn ... the last race of the day. Nervously he stared ahead at the finishing tape. Daniel and Jake stood at the far end of the course shouting encouragement. One of the teachers called out, 'On your marks. Get set. Go!' – and they were off.

Dave ran like the wind. All of a sudden he felt the tape stretch against his chest as he broke through. 'The winner. He's the winner!' Jake and Daniel could hardly believe it. All that training had paid off. Jake and Daniel jumped around clapping each other on the back, and then they both ran over to Dave and clapped him on the back too.

That evening, as the boys were putting up the tent, they decided to pin all three rosettes to the side of the tent door. They laid out the dog bait in the dish. Even Jake admitted that it looked quite appetizing. Dogger would have gobbled it down in seconds. They spent some time chatting about the races and about what they were going to do with the rest of the holidays. They even stayed awake until midnight for a feast, but not long after that they decided it was time for some sleep. The walkie-talkies were ready, so Jake decided to take first watch. However, when morning arrived and there was no sign of any dog. All three boys were quite fed up.

Just then Jake had an idea. 'How stupid I've been!' he exclaimed. The other boys looked at him strangely. 'Why didn't I think of it before!'

Jake ran up the road towards Number 6. Daniel and Dave followed him. Jake wondered if this was just a silly idea of his.

'What are you doing, Jake?' Daniel asked.

'Number 6 is that dog's home... not was. It doesn't know that the house has been sold. Dogger used to have hiding places all over our garden. Dogs can be good at hiding if they don't want to be found. That dog is still at Number 6. We should have realised that. Instead of setting up the tent at Joyce's we should have set it up at Number 6. That's where the dog is!'

'I think you're right,' Dave said. 'So where is it?'

Jake looked. 'Where would Dogger have hidden?' he asked himself. At first he couldn't see anywhere, but then he spotted the coal bunker. Instead of a shed this house had a large box at the back of the garden where the coal could be shovelled. Usually coal bunkers of this type had a large hatch near the bottom where the coal could be shovelled into a bucket. But the bunker looked empty from here, and there wasn't a door ... just a big dark hole in the side. Jake pointed at it and said, 'That would be a good place. It would actually make a perfect kennel.'

Dave and Daniel both nodded their heads in agreement. The more they looked at the bunker, the more they were certain that something was hiding there. Daniel whispered, 'It's the dog! I can see it. Look – there's a pair of eyes glinting at us.'

The three boys stared in astonishment. But what Daniel couldn't work out was why it hadn't eaten their food. Jake couldn't work it out either, 'There must be a reason,' he thought. Then Dave spotted something by the shrubbery. 'Is that a dog dish?'

Jake muttered, 'It's Dogger's dog dish.'

'I thought we had that,' Dave said puzzled.

'We have one of them. That dish over by the bush is another. I wondered why I couldn't find it in the garage. I was sure there had been two... and we used to have a lot more dog food too.'

Jake shook his head. It was all falling into place. Jumping off his seat, he ran down the road and through the door at Number 11. There was no sign of Tammy, but Mum was sitting in the kitchen, her hands cupped round a mug of coffee.

'No joy then, boys? That's a shame. I was sure you would have seen something.'

'Mum,' Jake said, 'we didn't see it because someone else fed the dog last night. I went to the garage to find Dogger's bowls yesterday. I only found one. There were only two tins of dog food in the cupboard.'

Mum looked surprised at that. 'Only two? I know I meant to get rid of them – but I never got round to it. There should have been at least five or six tins there. What happened to them?'

'Do you remember that Tammy was going through these boxes of Joyce's the other night?' Mum nodded. 'Well, all of a sudden Tammy left and I found a photo in the bin. Daniel and I recognised the dog, and Joyce said it must have belonged to the old man from Number 6.'

'Do you think Tammy has been feeding that dog?' Mum asked.

'Yes ... Dogger's bowl is sitting underneath the shrubbery at Number 6 right this minute.'

Mrs MacDonald nodded her head and sighed. 'I asked you if you were ready for another dog, Jake, and you said no. I asked Tammy the same question, and I almost had to scrape her off the ceiling because she was so excited. She thought I'd said we were getting one. She was so disappointed when I told her we weren't getting one just yet.'

Jake then turned to Dave and Daniel. 'I'm sure she's behind this.'

And then, from the top of the stairs, came a quiet voice, 'Yes. You're right. I am.'

'Tammy, love,' Mum exclaimed, as Tammy ran down the stairs in a flood of tears. 'Why did you keep it all a secret?'

'I don't know. I just felt like having a secret to myself. And I miss Dogger and wanted to look after this dog. She was so lonely.'

'She?' said Jake. 'I thought it was a he.'

'It's a she,' explained Tammy. 'On her collar she has a name tag, and it's Dora. I think that's a girl's name. Anyway... I've been looking after her since the yard sale. They took away her kennel and she's been sleeping in the coal bunker since then. I've been playing with her and looking after her, and she really likes me. It's just that when she's on her own she gets really bored. That's when she knocks over bins. Once or twice she's snuck into our garden, but she won't stay in Dogger's old kennel. I tried to get her to come over one night when you were all asleep.'

'You mean to say you've been wandering around Canterbury Place in your pyjamas in the middle of the night?' Mum had changed from being a little concerned to being quite annoyed, and maybe even angry.

Tammy had a very sorry expression on her face. Mum sighed.

'Well, there's only one thing for it. You're grounded for the rest of the weekend. In fact, you're not leaving this house until we leave for Edinburgh… unless it's to go to church on Sunday.' Mum heaved a sigh of relief. 'That dog appears to be nice natured … but I don't know what we are going to do about it.'

The following day being Sunday the MacDonald family were off to church

 again. The Sunday school was great fun so that even Tammy forgot her troubles. Joyce had laid out juice and snacks. Flowers decorated

the table in vases and there was even music playing in the background. Special hats had been made for the guests, and some other costumes were laid out at the side for later on. First of all Joyce wanted to tell a story from the gospel of Matthew, chapter 25. It was a story that Jesus had told to explain to people about what it was going to be like when he came back to earth for a second time.

'This story is about a wedding and some bridesmaids,' Joyce explained. 'Five of these bridesmaids were wise and five were foolish.

In Bible times bridesmaids had to accompany the bridegroom to the wedding. The bridegroom would arrive at the house at any time of the day or night and the bridesmaids would have to be ready to walk with him through the streets to the reception.

Weddings were great celebrations and everyone had a marvellous time, but only those who were invited by the family attended the celebration. That night, as soon as the bridesmaids heard the groom arriving, they all jumped to their feet. The wise bridesmaids had plenty of oil in their lamps. They were organised and ready to walk with the bridegroom. The five foolish bridesmaids did not have enough oil in their lamps to light them through the dark streets. Without lamps they wouldn't be able to find their way. They pleaded with the wise bridesmaids to give them some of their oil.

'We can't do that,' the girls said. 'We won't have enough oil for ourselves. Go and find a market stall or something and buy your own oil.'

With that the five foolish bridesmaids ran off to buy some oil, while the five wise bridesmaids made their way to the wedding with the groom.

By the time the other bridesmaids had arrived at the celebration, the doors had been locked and they couldn't get in however hard they tried.'

Now as Joyce went over to pick up the remaining costumes, she asked the class a question. 'Can anyone tell me what this story means? Why did Jesus tell it to us?'

Jake raised his hand to reply. 'Yes, Jake, what do you think the reason is?'

'Jesus wanted to tell us to get ready for

heaven. Heaven is going to be like a great celebration, but only those who love and trust in Jesus will be allowed to go. The five wise bridesmaids were ready. The five foolish ones weren't. If we want to go to heaven we have to be ready.'

'Well done, Jake,' Joyce exclaimed. 'We must ask God to forgive our sins. It is because Jesus died for us that we can be forgiven. If we die without being forgiven, we won't be allowed in heaven, and we will be separated from God's love for ever.'

Joyce then asked the class, 'Have you given your hearts to Jesus? Are you ready to join this wonderful celebration called Heaven and Eternal life? Think about this, and let the feast begin.' With that she handed Tammy a bride's veil and seated her at the top of the table with Daniel, the pretend groom. He was dressed in a very grand cloak. Everyone else either wore a hat or a veil. Joyce had gone to a lot of work, and everything had turned out really well. Joyce and some of the other teachers served juice and snacks and everybody had a really good time.

As they waved goodbye to Joyce after church she smiled at Jake and winked. 'Your mum told me about the dog. I'll see you both this afternoon. I might just have the answer to all your problems.'

Jake looked puzzled. 'What is she on about?' he wondered.

That afternoon Joyce called in to the MacDonald household. Jake couldn't work out why she was holding a very shabby blanket, or why there was a strange man in a uniform standing beside her.

'This is my friend Scott,' Joyce announced. 'He's from the RSPCA and comes to church with me sometimes.'

Scott shook hands with everyone and then asked where they could find this dog he'd been hearing about. Dad pointed towards Number 6, while Joyce explained to the others what they planned to do.

'Scott reckons that between us we can get that dog to leave Number 6 and make it's home with you guys... if you want that?'

Joyce looked at Mrs MacDonald, and Mrs MacDonald looked at Tammy and Jake. Jake smiled and Tammy let out a great big cheer.

'Right then,' Joyce said. 'That's all the answer I need. I'll go and help Scott. I've got something he really needs.'

Jake wondered what Joyce was on about but minutes later they saw Joyce and Scott coaxing a rather bedraggled looking grey dog from the coal bunker at Number 6 to the back garden at Number 11. Joyce was dragging the smelly old blanket in front of the dog as she headed for the back of the garden.

'What on earth is she doing with that?' Mrs MacDonald asked.

Dad coughed politely, and then he explained. 'Well... you see... Tammy had already told us that the dog doesn't like Dogger's kennel, so Joyce had this idea that we could use the Morris Minor instead.'

Mum stared at Joyce as she opened the back door of the little car and flung the dirty old dog blanket inside it. The old grey dog leapt in after it and immediately looked quite at home.

'Well,' she said, as she looked at her beloved old car. 'Luxury kennels, whatever next?'

Dad gave her a hug. 'I knew you would understand. This way you keep the car and can see it every day and it is being put to a good use too!'

Mum sighed and then nodded her head in agreement.

Everyone cheered and the old grey dog barked and wagged its tail.

'How did you find that blanket, Joyce? The dog is obviously very attached to it?' Mrs MacDonald asked.

'Easy. I remembered who had bought the kennel at the yard sale. I was sure there had been an old blanket inside it. I phoned them up yesterday, and apparently they had cleaned out the kennel and the blanket was sitting in the garage waiting for the next bin day. I just got it in time.'

'But who is going to look after her while we go to the wedding?' Tammy asked.

Joyce volunteered. 'I'll even camp out on the grass like the boys if the dog needs some company.'

'That's sorted then,' Mr MacDonald exclaimed. 'What an unusual Sunday this has been. Tammy, see if you can get that dog to make friends with Jake now,' Dad urged. 'If there's time before we head off to Edinburgh tomorrow, I'll see if I can get rid of Dogger's kennel. Do you know anyone who wants one?' he asked Joyce.

Joyce shrugged her shoulders, 'Why not use it as a coal bunker?' she laughed.

And as the adults made their way inside for a cup of tea, Tammy and Jake took

some treats over to the new MacDonald dog. 'Dora's a funny name,' Jake exclaimed.

'So was Dogger!' Tammy argued.

Jake nodded. The  MacDonald's were just going to have to put up with strangely named dogs. With a bright blue ball in her hand, Tammy persuaded Dora to come out and play. By the end of the evening it seemed as if she had always been there.

The following morning the MacDonalds were up bright and early, with their cases packed and in the car.

Joyce came to see them off and to make sure that Dora wouldn't do a runner again. But Mrs MacDonald exclaimed how she'd never seen a dog look so happy inside a car.

As they drove off, leaving Canterbury Place behind them it wasn't long before

Tammy began counting the days until their journey home. Somehow Dora had taken the place of bridesmaids' dresses and Tammy was anxious to get back to their new pet.

Jake thought about mystery dogs, secret drawers, sports days and the party, and sighed. What a lot had been going on. He remembered the discussion that they'd had about weddings and loyalty and love, and as everyone else seemed busy with their own thoughts Jake decided now was a good time for a quiet prayer.

Jake prayed for Jen and Philip as they

made this really big change in their lives. He thought about what his dad had said to him about praying for his own marriage.

'Maybe I'll be like Joyce and not get married or maybe God will show me who he wants me to marry.' Jake thought it was strange thinking like this. He really wasn't sure if he wanted to get married at all. 'Help me to be loyal to you, Lord Jesus,' he prayed, as more motorway signposts whizzed by. 'Help me to make decisions that please you in whatever I do. Help me to love you and to love others before myself. Amen.'

Think about it?

Questions: What does loyalty mean? Are you loyal to others? Are you a true friend of Jesus? If you are then what sort of person should you marry? Have you ever thought about who you might marry? Do people have to get married? What does it mean to be steadfast? Is it hard to be a steadfast Christian? Who can help us be steadfast?

Answers: Loyalty means being a true friend, dependable and faithful. If you are a true friend to others they can trust and rely on you. You won't talk behind their backs and you will put others before yourself. If you are a true friend of Jesus you will put him first. You will follow God's laws and trust and love Jesus Christ.

If you are a true friend of Jesus and if you marry, then you should marry someone who loves Jesus most of all. Pray about who you might marry and ask God to help you make the right decision. God may have better plans for you than marriage. God's plans for you are the best plans. If he doesn't plan for you to get married then you shouldn't. You should ask God to make it clear to you what he wants you to do in every situation in your life.

Ask God to be your guide throughout your life and your helper in everything. Ask him to protect you and your family from sin so that you may all be steadfast and immovable in your love to God. God is steadfast and dependable always. He can help us to be the people that he wants us to be.

When people die in order to defend something that is true and good they sacrifice their lives for a good thing. Jesus sacrificed his life for his people. Jesus was obedient to God even unto death. Jesus was the only truly perfect sacrifice. He died in our place. Jesus the perfect one, who never sinned, died instead of disobedient people like us.

For God so loved the world that he gave his only son that whoever believes in him should not perish but have everlasting life. John 3:16.

Live for Jesus. He died for you.

Stories from Canterbury Place

The other title in this series:

The Big Green Tree at No. 11
Tammy and Jake learn about Life and Death.
ISBN: 1-85792-731-1

The Dark Blue Bike at No. 17
Tammy and Jake learn about
Friendship and Bullying.
ISBN: 1-85792-732-X

The Deep Black Pond at No. 12
Tammy and Jake learn about
Health and Sickness.
ISBN: 1-85792-733-8

Author Information

Catherine Mackenzie is a Christian writer and Sunday school teacher from Scotland.

As a child Catherine never needed much persuasion to read a story - although her parents had to come up with a variety of creative ideas to persuade her to do extra arithmetic.

As well as the Canterbury place series she has written several biographies for young readers. She also has a series of illustrated books published for younger children on issues such as: A new baby, A new home, Going to school and Going to the doctor.

'It is great to be able to do something I enjoy in order to introduce children to Jesus and God's word. It's a privilege to be involved in God's ministry of words.'

CHRISTIAN FOCUS

Staying faithful - Reaching out!

Christian Focus Publications publishes books for adults and children under its three main imprints: Christian Focus; Mentor and Christian Heritage. Our books reflect that God's word is reliable and Jesus is the way to know him, and live forever with him.

Our children's publication list includes a Sunday school curriculum that covers pre-school to early teens; puzzle and activity books. We also publish personal and family devotional titles, biographies and inspirational stories that children will love.

If you are looking for quality Bible teaching for children then we have an excellent range of Bible story and age specific theological books.

From pre-school to teenage fiction, we have it covered!

Find us at our web page: www.christianfocus.com